DISNEP
THE SORCERER'S APPRENTICE

ARCANA CABANA
CATALOGUE

Please be advised that the items found within this
catalogue are not actually for sale. This is a parody
for collectors of unique and magical gifts of all ages.

Written by Jack Palacios

Copyright © 2010 Disney Enterprises, Inc.
JERRY BRUCKHEIMER FILMS™ and JERRY BRUCKHEIMER FILMS Tree Logo™ are all trademarks.
All rights reserved. Unauthorized use is prohibited.
Illustrations by Gregory Hill, Dean Tschetter, Tani Kunitake, and Miles Teves

The Last Unicorn © Francis G. Mayer/CORBIS

Visit www.disneybooks.com
Printed in the United States of America
First Edition
1 3 5 7 9 10 8 6 4 2
V381-8386-5-10105
Library of Congress Catalog Card Number on file.
ISBN 978-1-4231-2691-1

SUSTAINABLE
FORESTRY
INITIATIVE

Certified Chain of Custody
35% Certified Forests,
65% Certified Fiber Sourcing
www.sfiprogram.org

WELCOME TO

· ARCANA CABANA LTD ·

DISNEP PRESS
New York

ARCANA CABANA

Dear Valued Customer,

Thank you for your interest in the Arcana Cabana. It warms my heart to know that there are still men and women with interests and tastes so similar to mine. In this day and age, it is rare to find an individual who can appreciate the unique, the unusual, and shall we say, the obscure.

For those of you lucky enough to live close by, or perhaps to be planning a trip to New York City, I encourage you to stop by the shop. I've spent a lot of time collecting the items that line the shelves, cover the floors, and fill the bookcases. Whether it is one of my personal favorites, such as a prized unicorn horn, or a beautiful ring from my own collection, each item is truly special. The stories and histories you will read in the catalogue seem the stuff of fiction but are in truth, fact . . . for the most part. It was my dream, upon opening the store years ago, to bring a touch of the Old World into the new. I feel that I have accomplished this task but leave it up to you, the customer (after all, you are always right), to see if I struck true.

Happy shopping—and beware; beyond
these pages, there may be dragons. . . .

—Balthazar Blake, proprietor

HISTORY OF THE
ARCANA CABANA

Like many places in New York City, the Arcana Cabana's history started long before its doors opened in 1888. Nestled in the downtown section of Manhattan, the building as it stands now began as the private residence of a young doctor and his wife in 1850. Prior to that, the records are less clear, although references have been found linking it at one time to a butcher shop, a funeral home, and even a flower shop.

Fresh out of medical school, with dreams of helping the poor, the young doctor took his family fortune and spent it all on the building. It would, he hoped, be the perfect spot for him to start his new family and practice. But alas, as so many dreams do, this one did not turn out as planned. His wife never bore the children he had hoped for, and the practice was feared by the locals. They complained that strange lights could be seen coming from the basement window and that sounds echoed through the narrow alley in front of the building at all hours of the night. It was even said that the doctor himself, while he lived there for over three decades, did not age a day. The only sign of his passing years was a cane he was sometimes seen to use. When his wife left the world, the doctor, who had long ago stopped practicing, lost the will to maintain the building. He let it fall into disrepair, and by 1888, when it became the Arcana Cabana, it was a dusty shell of a place where few dared to tread.

According to housing ledgers, the building was purchased in foreclosure in 1888 for a mere $15.00 by one Balthazar Blake (clearly not the same Balthazar who greeted you on the opposite page, as that would make him well over a hundred years old!). Blake had recently arrived in the United States from Great Britain and immediately took it upon himself to fix the place and restore it to its original grandeur. By the end of the year, the renovations were complete and the Arcana Cabana, home of antiquities, unusual gifts, and obscurities, opened its doors to the public.

STRANGE HAPPENINGS AT THE
ARCANA CABANA

The store was not an instant success by any means. The neighbors were still wary—this time with perhaps a bit more reason. Blake was not the most sociable of figures. He mainly kept to himself, opening the store at odd hours and sometimes not at all. And the items with which he filled the store were worrisome to some more superstitious New Yorkers. Combined with his own "unique" style—he was always seen in a long leather jacket that smelled of ancient and faraway lands and a strange pointed hat which could, when casting a shadow, appear almost like a witch's hat—it was no surprise that response to the store was lukewarm at first.

However, over time, the Arcana Cabana became a destination in its own right. People who needed to get their hands on special gifts or who were curious to find out more about loved ones, bosses, family, etc., would make their way through the front door, the tinkling sound of a tiny bell announcing their presence as they sought out their prizes. Blake himself became a more stable member of the community—although

he ended up disappearing for quite some time.

His great-grandson, another Balthazar Blake and the current proprietor, came to run the store in 1998 and did little to change or update the look or inventory. It continued to operate with little fuss or fanfare until one spring day in 2000. On that particular day, the store was said to be the site of a robbery attempt. While nothing was reported stolen, numerous eyewitness accounts mentioned seeing strange flashes of light and hearing loud crashes and thuds. One woman even claimed that she snuck up, and, peeking through the window, saw Balthazar throw what she called a "lightning ball" at

another man wearing a black hat and fancy suit. Another bystander, this time a member of a school field trip who had wandered into the store accidentally, says that he saw Balthazar get sucked into a large urn. The student stated hysterically that he had been caught between two sorcerers who told him he was "the one." He even claimed Balthazar forced a dragon to walk on his hand. But of course, these are just tales—part of the lore that goes along with a store of such unique character and long history. Or are they?

If the reports of that action-packed day are to be believed, Balthazar was indeed trapped in an urn and was not seen again until ten years later to the day. On that fateful morning, the lights were once again turned on in the Arcana Cabana and luckily for us, they remain on, the store a bright spot for unique gift givers of all ages.

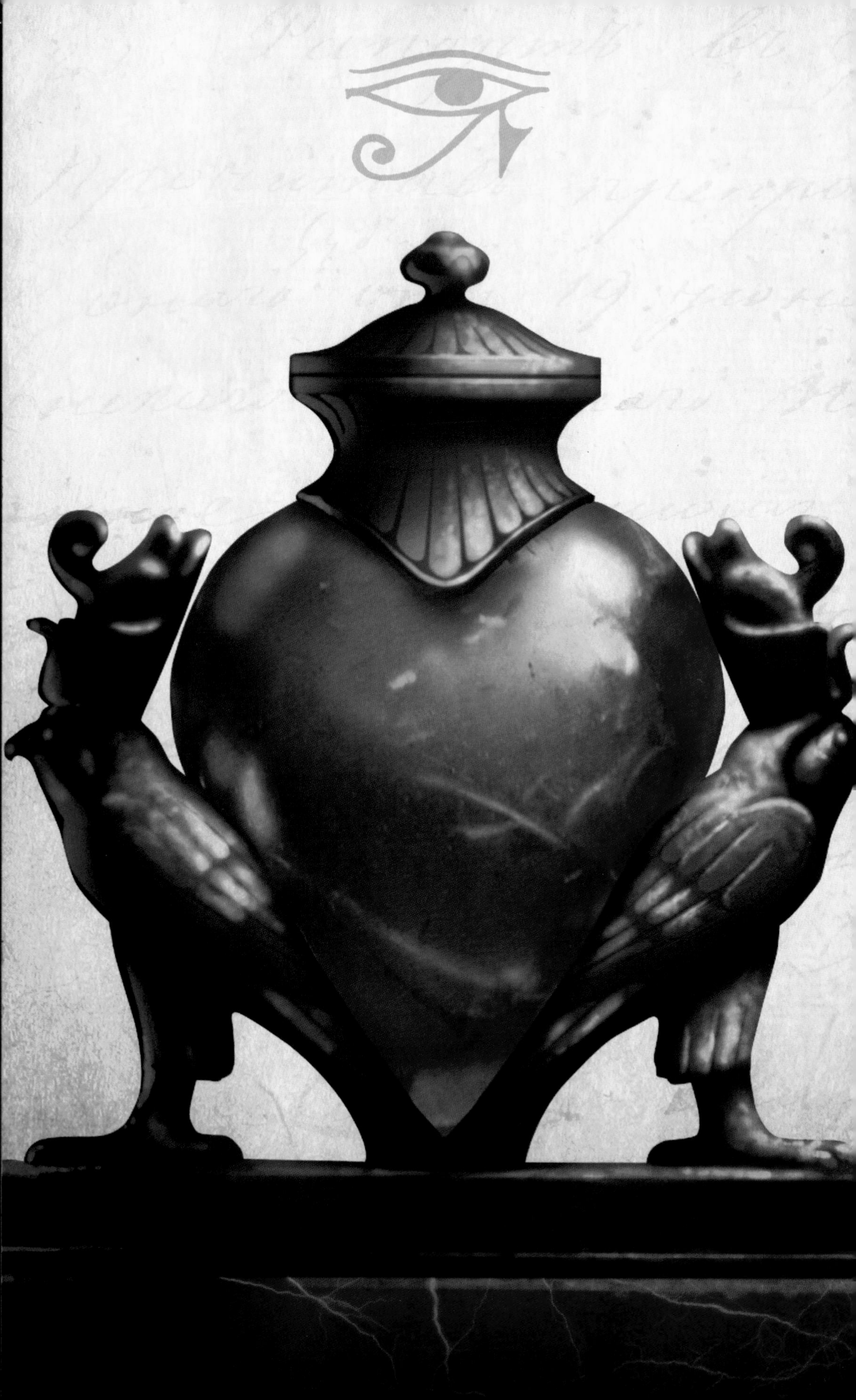

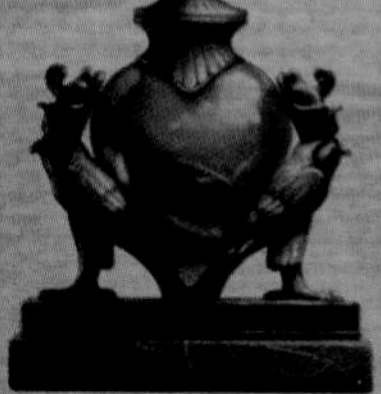

CLEOPATRA'S HEART

How do you put a price tag on love? In the case of this finely crafted heart-shaped jar, the task is not quite so difficult. Encased in the red transparent glass is not only the heart of the last Egyptian pharaoh, Cleopatra, but that of her true love, Mark Antony.

As the legend goes, their love was so great that as long as their hearts were always together the love they shared would last in this life and beyond. This was made possible when their hearts were placed in this jar, the golden birds on each side serving as protectors from the viscious asps that struck Cleopatra down.

Marble base, gold birds, and lid, plus two hearts make this a steal at **$75,000**.

TRAPPING URN

One of the more popular items in the store, the Chinese Trapping Urn is far more useful than it first appears. Have a pesky relative you want to be rid of for a decade? Or perhaps your neighbor is just too loud? If so, one of these highly detailed and beautifully illustrated urns is just the thing. Whoever opens the lid will be trapped inside for exactly ten years. And if you simply want a lovely decorative piece, these urns feature panoramic drawings of such "light" topics as war, death, and the underworld in a variety of colors and sizes sure to complement any decor.

$60.05 for one/**$100.10** for a set of two

GARGOYLE

Just like the one that stands watch outside the Arcana Cabana, our 100% authentic gargoyles bring to mind those found on the Cathédrale Notre Dame de Paris. Useful watchdogs, these come in a variety of stones, such as marble and terra-cotta, as well as a variety of sizes to fit your needs. For an additional cost, we can custom order to fit faces, styles, or even engravings of your choosing.

Terra-cotta: 3 ft. **$450**/6 ft. **$800**
Marble: 3 ft. **$10,000**/6 ft. **$20,000**
Custom options: Please call to order

BARGAIN ITEM

SNAKES

Are you looking for a unique way to express your love? Are you always at each other's throats? Either way, you'll want to take a bite out of these Kissing Snakes. We carry a large-scale model as well as a variety of smaller species so you can pick your poison.

$874.99
(On sale; originally priced at $1,500)

TURBINE

Going green? Or has your turbine broken down on you again? You're in luck! Here at the Arcana Cabana we have a one-of-a-kind, brass-plated turbine just waiting for a new home.

Yours for the once-in-a-lifetime price of **$50.25**
(No refunds. Because, face it, who really needs a turbine?)

 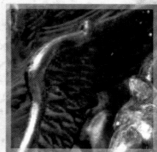 

GRIFFIN

Do you suffer from a god complex? Is Napoléon your hero? In your opinion, should people bow down to you? If you answered yes to any of these questions, this griffin MUST be placed in the front of your temple—sorry, we mean your home. Historically a symbol of great power and divinity, no great person went without a griffin in his or her residence. Made of bronze with detailed etchings on the face and wings, these four-foot-long, three-foot-tall beauties are a must.

$1,829.50
(Will also accept other forms of payment in trade if you are currently unable to find your stash of cash.)

WOODEN BELL

An early version of what would one day be the Liberty Bell has arrived at the Arcana Cabana. It was found to have some flaws as aged metal is not a great sound conductor. Nevertheless, it will make for interesting dinner conversation or, if you are feeling chilled, the wooden frame would make great firewood.

The cost? Whatever change you have! Canadian money, silver dollars, and Sacagewea coins also accepted.

RAM SKULL

Newly arrived! This piece is a wonderful wall hanging, sure to inspire great conversation. If you are looking for something that is more multipurpose, hang this by the front door and you have a perfect coatrack.

$55.55

HUMAN SKULL

Are you always searching for the perfect centerpiece? Something that will keep people smiling? Then how about this rare collection of ceramic human skulls that replicate those found at a burial site in the Congo? They also work well as candleholders.

Set of two: **$25.15**

CEREMONIAL WALL HANGING

Did last year's Halloween party get out of hand? Is there a hole in your wall you need to cover? Look no further. This ceremonial mask is two feet wide and makes a perfect cover for that eyesore.

$43.45 (Free gift with purchase: set of four matching coasters—for next year's party!)

DECORATIVE VASES

To keep the floor from being jealous of the walls, check out this collection of oversized decorative vases that come in a variety of colors and shapes. Just be sure to check inside. The Arcana Cabana cannot be held responsible for any bugs or demons that may lurk there.

Price varies. Please call for quote.

AZTEC CEREMONIAL BLADE

Looking for the perfect gift for your culinary counterpart? Is a golden anniversary around the corner? Here is the only present you'll need. This beautifully detailed gold ceremonial blade is inlaid with rubies, sapphires, and emeralds. Forged roughly 600 years ago at the height of the Aztec Empire, this was at one time used for sacrificing young maids to angry gods but is now a mean cake cutter. In fact, this item is so valuable we can only show you a drawing. For further details, please contact us at the store.

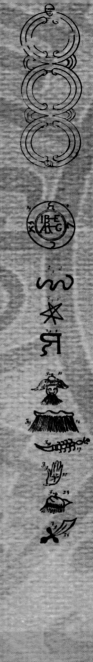

SWORDS

Wondering how to protect your pricey investments? Never fear; the Arcana Cabana is here to help. These two swords come with their very own set of authentic wooden scabbards (be mindful of splinters!). Each also features a crest that dates back to the age of King Arthur—or so they say.

$1,500 for one/**$2,800** for the pair

MAGIC BOOKS

Are you looking to impress your literary lady? Or do you simply have a lot of empty bookshelves and only magazines? Our library covers everything from magic spells (How do you change your enemy into a porcupine? What exactly *does* go into a love potion?) to histories of ancient peoples. This collection is guaranteed to make you look and feel like a professor of both magical and everyday studies. First editions priced higher.

$6.99 to **$600.99**, depending on the volume

PIRATE RAPIERS

Thought to have been used by the infamous Pirate Lord Jack Sparrow, these lightweight, diamond-tipped rapiers are unique and deadly. Will look lovely placed by a fireplace or near the door. After all, you never know when you'll need protection!

$10,500

HOLY GRAIL BOOKENDS

The Arcana Cabana has finally found the Holy Grail . . . of bookends.
These detailed pieces are a must for any mantel or bookshelf where you
want to display your treasures. Our magic books look exceptionally
nice between the two knights.

$313.33

Arcana Cabana / Fashion Piece

WIZARD'S HAT

One of the most prized and priceless items in the store, this Wizard's Hat is rumored to have served as inspiration in the creation of one of the most powerful sorcerers in the world—a mouse. Fanciful and fantastic, the hat is a handcrafted, unique item made with imported cloth. Embellished with two stars and a crescent moon, the stitching was done in 100% pure gold on silk. You can own a piece of magical history by purchasing this amazing and inspiring hat.

Price depends on purchaser.

CLOCK

Did you make a fool of yourself in front of your crush? Were you late for work—again? If you are wishing you could turn back time, wish no more! This amazing time-travel clock allows you to fix any problems you've had in the past twelve hours by simply turning the hand to the appropriate hour.

The clock has been in such high demand that it is no longer available at *this* time. Maybe someone will return it in his *own* time.

VINTAGE FILM REELS

Fresh from the vaults of the Walt Disney Studios, these one-of-a-kind film reels hold the original footage of the classic animated film *Fantasia*. Only released in this version once, in 1941, the magic nevertheless remains and, on the rare occasion, takes over. The previous owner bequeathed these items to the Arcana Cabana after complaints of them taking flight. We have only witnessed this event once but assure our customers there is no danger from injuries due to the low-flying objects.

Please contact store for quote.

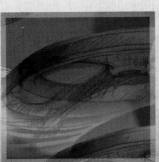

NESTING DOLLS

Looking for a gift that is layered? This is the item for you! Our nesting doll is in fact four different dolls placed inside one another. Collectively known as the Grimhold, each doll is made of a different element and features a beautifully rendered illustration of some of the most powerful sorcerers ever rumored to exist: Maxim Horvath, Sun Lok, Abigail Smith (She looks sweet, but this little girl was reportedly the cause of the Salem witch trials.), and finally, Morgana, the most evil sorceress of all. It has been said that the dolls actually keep the sorcerers imprisoned inside. If the sorcerers were to be released, they would be capable of much destruction. But that is just a rumor. Really.

Price negotiable.

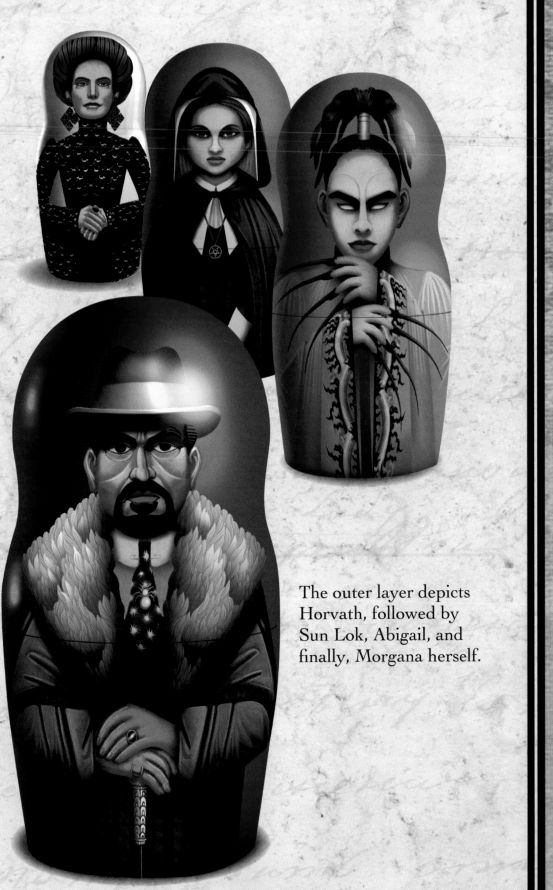

The outer layer depicts Horvath, followed by Sun Lok, Abigail, and finally, Morgana herself.

GRIMHOLD CASE

FREE GIFT WITH PURCHASE

WHILE SUPPLIES LAST!

This carrying case makes bringing your Grimhold to various functions a breeze. Compact and lightweight, the case fits in overhead compartments, so you won't have to worry about that extra luggage fee at the airport. Just be careful not to let the sorcerers out!

*Note: not to scale

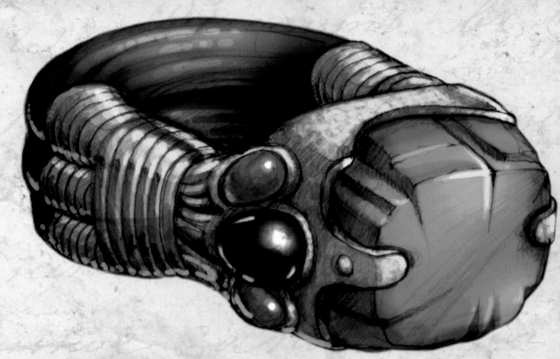

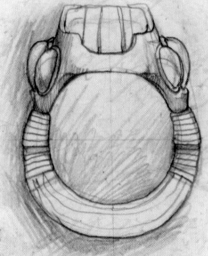

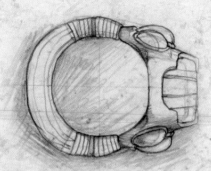

EMERALD RING

Legend tells of a man whose power was so great that those around him feared he would grow out of control. He promised that his power would only be used for good, but none believed these words true. The great Merlin then appeared and forged a ring of the strongest gold and the purest emerald to hold this man's power and insure his control. Greatness is given to the one who wears the ring, or so the stories say, but if placed on a finger of an unworthy person, the ring will turn to dust.

This ring of myth is a myth no more and now sits in the vault of the Arcana Cabana! Last worn by the store's proprietor, Balthazar Blake, it is an item that will only be given to the worthy. Please inquire in person if you are interested. There *will* be a test.

ONYX RING I

Another legend tells of a man whose desire for power was so great, he was willing to sacrifice his soul to obtain it. This man spurned the help of the great Merlin and set out to craft his own ring to control the elements and harness his dark magic. The first attempt resulted in a ring made of onyx and amethyst. The beetle etched in the onyx is inlaid with the amethyst, its details simple. It is said that when the ring is worn by a person with a black heart, the purple glows and casts a shadow on those standing near.

Sold out at this time. Please check back to see if inventory has been replenished.

ONYX RING II

Later attempts at creating a ring strong enough to contain such dark magic resulted in a style similar to the original. Once again crafted from the darkest onyx, this ring has silver etching. This combination of metal and gem creates a nearly indestructible item. Many have tried to destroy it, but it is now securely locked away in the Arcana Cabana vault. We have included this ring as a warning to those who find similar ones. Be wary. They may look like innocent pieces of jewelry, but there is absolutely *nothing* innocent about them.

Price not applicable.

MERLIN'S RING

Arthurian legend is never complete without mention of the great and powerful sorcerer Merlin. A vital member of King Arthur's court, Merlin was a man ahead of his time. Capable of the greatest magic, an avid inventor, and supposedly a skilled marksman, Merlin's reach extended beyond the territories of Arthur's rule.

It is said that Merlin had three apprentices who helped him craft his magic, but he also had an archenemy—Morgana. To protect his power and ward off the forces of darkness, he crafted his own ring. When he lost his life, it ended up in the hands of his apprentices.

A dragon with eyes and crest made of the strongest emerald, the silver ring also has intricate detailing on the wings and body. When it finds its rightful owner, an inscription will appear on the inside: *Take me up, cast me away.* It will then curl itself around the owner's finger, making it one with the sorcerer descended from the great Merlin himself—the Prime Merlinean.

Currently only one in existence. Please contact D. Stutler if curious.

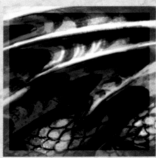

CHINA

Are you entertaining royalty? Have a tea party planned for ten? Then you need to own a set of our very finest china. We offer three settings from three different times and places in history. One is sure to be perfect for you.

BLUE CHINA

One of our rarer collections, the blue in this pattern represents the period in China's dynasties when the only dye available was indigo. This lasted for only four years and during that time a total of sixty sets were made. This is one of the last remaining collections.

$24,000

RED CHINA

Said to be made with a dye that combines 50% pure dragon's blood and 50% crushed pearl (but you can't always trust what you hear), these pieces are detailed with the classic toile de Jouy pattern that originated in France in the 1700s.

$500

BABY PRINT

If you are a bit more whimsical with your dishware, this tea set from Holland is just the thing. The coffeepot, sugar bowl, milk jug, and matching set of six cups and saucers have a lovely pattern of a young boy frolicking. This is one of the last remaining sets of its kind. Don't miss out!

$12,000

ENCANTUS

Are you looking for a way to impress a special person in your life? Do you want to make sure your skin is perfectly smooth on the night of the big dance? Or is there a dark sorcerer trying to make sure you don't succeed in saving the world? If you are of pure heart and soul, the Encantus is the solution to all your problems!

Full of spells and magic, this book is not merely a primer for young apprentices interested in learning sorcery. It also details the history of sorcery—with beautiful illustrations and a melodic narrative. The pages have been painstakingly rendered in this replica of the original, which is said to reside in the safe hands of the Prime Merlinean himself.

For price, please inquire by phone or in person.

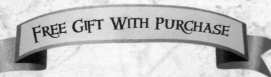

FREE GIFT WITH PURCHASE

POCKET ENCANTUS

Perfect when you want to take the magic to go, this palm-sized book will open to reveal all your spells. Magic is literally at your fingertips!

HORVATH'S ENCANTUS

Are you hoping to take over the world? Do you prefer the shadows to the light? If so, please don't contact us again. This item is displayed as yet another warning. It, too, is an Encantus, but rather than teaching the magic of light, it was used to teach Morgana's followers the path of darkness. Notice the notched wood cover. It was created from the bark of a tree found near Morgana's lair and has clearly absorbed her evil touch. In the center, a beetle serves as a warning to those who dare open the cover and turn the pages inside. The four jewels with their heavy clasps were forged of metal and fire and have been said to burn when touched.

This is a replica. If you see such a book, please return it to Arcana Cabana, c/o Balthazar Blake or Dave Stutler.

UNICORN HORN

One of our most prized possessions, this is the skull of the animal that inspired the set of seven tapestries called *The Hunt of the Unicorn*. Crafted in the 1500s in either Brussels or Liège, the tapestries depict one unicorn's capture and eventual taming.

That same unicorn's skull now adorns a wall of the Arcana Cabana. There it has watched over visitors and owners alike, powerful and beautiful in its mystery.

Due to a minor incident in which the horn was used as a weapon in a rumored sorcerers' battle here at the shop, the item has been discounted.

$101,005
(Will negotiate trade for unicorn skull of the famed Last Unicorn.)

SERPENT EGG

This handblown glass piece is a perfect accessory for the refined home. Said to be a replica of an egg that hatched or released the evil Morgana from her capture (She is no longer free, so no need to worry—yet.), it is made of red glass and appears, in the right light, to pulse with an unknown energy.

$125.00

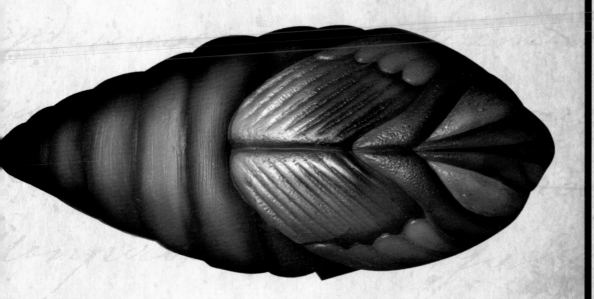

BUTTERFLY EGG

This is another must-have piece for anyone of discerning taste. Handcrafted from bamboo, the details etched on the object portray the wings of the butterfly that waits inside to be born. The colors are bright and cheerful, and we are sure nothing but good can be brought forth from its wooden confines.

$75.00

PHANTOM II

Built in 1935 as part of the Rolls-Royce Phantom II line of automobiles, this is one of the few remaining Phantoms left in such pristine condition. The bodywork is unique in that it was crafted by an individual coach builder picked by the owner. In this case, the detailing is exquisite, with a two-tone, gray-over-black combination and a leather interior. The two-door business coupe, with an extra boot compartment for carrying golf clubs (if you are heading to the links), has a six-cylinder engine and four-speed manual transmission that allow for great power under the hood. The engine (called the Merlin) used in later Phantom models was the same as the one found in the Spitfire and Mustang planes that flew in World War II.

$375,000

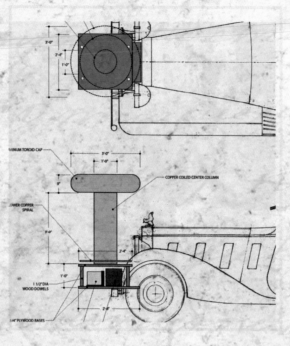

PHANTOM II WITH TESLA COIL

If you are looking for a little extra boost for your engine, why not think about adding your very own set of Tesla coils to the front of your car? That way, if you ever find yourself in the middle of a great sorcerers' battle, you can deflect and reflect plasma bolts while riding in style.

Price varies. Please contact Arcana Cabana motors division for details.

ARCANA CABANA
ORDER FORM

Tell us what you want . . .

_____

_____

_____

_____

_____

_____

_____

_____

_____

_____

. . . and we'll deliver it
before the year's end.

TOTAL CHARGES: